THE
BROKEN WINGS

KAHLIL GIBRAN

THE
Broken
Wings

translated from the Arabic by

ANTHONY R. FERRIS

THE CITADEL PRESS • NEW YORK

To my beloved wife and son
CARMEN and CURLY
Anthony R Ferris

Distributed to the Trade
by BOOK SALES, INC.
New York

DESIGNED BY ROSLYN HELD
INITIALS AND DECORATIONS BY JEANYEE WONG

Dedication

To the one who stares at the sun with glazed eyes and grasps the fire with untrembling fingers and hears the spiritual tune of Eternity behind the clamorous shrieking of the blind. To M.E.H. I dedicate this book.

GIBRAN

Contents

FOREWORD

 WAS EIGHTEEN
years of age when love opened my eyes with its magic
rays and touched my spirit for the first time with its
fiery fingers, and Selma Karamy was the first woman
who awakened my spirit with her beauty and led me
into the garden of high affection, where days pass
like dreams and nights like weddings.

Selma Karamy was the one who taught me to
worship beauty by the example of her own beauty
and revealed to me the secret of love by her affection;
she was the one who first sang to me the poetry of
real life.

Every young man remembers his first love and tries to recapture that strange hour, the memory of which changes his deepest feeling and makes him so happy in spite of all the bitterness of its mystery.

In every young man's life there is a "Selma" who appears to him suddenly while in the spring of life and transforms his solitude into happy moments and fills the silence of his nights with music.

I was deeply engrossed in thought and contemplation and seeking to understand the meaning of nature and the revelation of books and scriptures when I heard LOVE whispered into my ears through Selma's lips. My life was a coma, empty like that of Adam's in Paradise, when I saw Selma standing before me like a column of light. She was the Eve of my heart who filled it with secrets and wonders and made me understand the meaning of life.

The first Eve led Adam out of Paradise by her own will, while Selma made me enter willingly into the paradise of pure love and virtue by her sweetness and love; but what happened to the first man also happened to me, and the fiery sword which chased Adam out of Paradise was like the one which frightened me by its glittering edge and forced me away from the paradise of my love without having disobeyed any order or tasted the fruit of the forbidden tree.

Today, after many years have passed, I have nothing left out of that beautiful dream except painful memories flapping like invisible wings around me, filling the depths of my heart with sorrow, and bringing tears to my eyes; and my beloved, beautiful Selma, is dead and nothing is left to commemorate her except my broken heart and a tomb surrounded by cypress trees. That tomb and this heart are all that is left to bear witness of Selma.

The silence that guards the tomb does not reveal God's secret in the obscurity of the coffin, and the rustling of the branches whose roots suck the body's elements do not tell the mysteries of the grave, but the agonized sighs of my heart announce to the living the drama which love, beauty, and death have performed.

Oh, friends of my youth who are scattered in the city of Beirut, when you pass by that cemetery near the pine forest, enter it silently and walk slowly so the tramping of your feet will not disturb the slumber of the dead, and stop humbly by Selma's tomb and greet the earth that encloses her corpse and mention my name with a deep sigh and say to yourself, "Here, all the hopes of Gibran, who is living as a prisoner of love beyond the seas, were buried. On this spot he lost his happiness, drained his tears, and forgot his smile."

By that tomb grows Gibran's sorrow together with the cypress trees, and above the tomb his spirit flickers every night commemorating Selma, joining the branches of the trees in sorrowful wailing, mourning and lamenting the going of Selma, who, yesterday, was a beautiful tune on the lips of life and today is a silent secret in the bosom of the earth.

Oh, comrades of my youth! I appeal to you in the names of those virgins whom your hearts have loved, to lay a wreath of flowers on the forsaken tomb of my beloved, for the flowers you lay on Selma's tomb are like falling drops of dew from the eyes of dawn on the leaves of a withering rose.

SILENT SORROW

Y NEIGHBORS,
you remember the dawn of youth with pleasure and regret its passing; but I remember it like a prisoner who recalls the bars and shackles of his jail. You speak of those years between infancy and youth as a golden era free from confinement and cares, but I call those years an era of silent sorrow which dropped as a seed into my heart and grew with it and could find no outlet to the world of knowledge and wisdom until love came and opened the heart's doors and lighted its corners. Love provided me with a tongue

and tears. You people remember the gardens and orchids and the meeting places and street corners that witnessed your games and heard your innocent whispering; and I remember, too, the beautiful spot in North Lebanon. Every time I close my eyes I see those valleys full of magic and dignity and those mountains covered with glory and greatness trying to reach the sky. Every time I shut my ears to the clamor of the city I hear the murmur of the rivulets and the rustling of the branches. All those beauties which I speak of now and which I long to see, as a child longs for his mother's breast, wounded my spirit, imprisoned in the darkness of youth, as a falcon suffers in its cage when it sees a flock of birds flying freely in the spacious sky. Those valleys and hills fired my imagination, but bitter thoughts wove round my heart a net of hopelessness.

Every time I went to the fields I returned disappointed, without understanding the cause of my disappointment. Every time I looked at the gray sky I felt my heart contract. Every time I heard the singing of the birds and babbling of the spring I suffered without understanding the reason for my suffering. It is said that unsophistication makes a man empty and that emptiness makes him carefree. It may be true among those who were born dead and who exist like frozen corpses; but the sensitive boy who feels much and knows little is the most unfortunate creature under the sun, because he is torn by two forces. The first force elevates him and shows him the beauty of existence through a cloud of dreams; the second ties him down to the earth and fills his eyes with dust and overpowers him with fears and darkness.

Solitude has soft, silky hands, but with strong fingers it grasps the heart and makes it ache with sorrow. Solitude is the ally of sorrow as well as a companion of spiritual exaltation.

The boy's soul undergoing the buffeting of sorrow is like a white lily just unfolding. It trembles before the breeze and opens its heart to daybreak and folds its leaves back when the shadow of night comes. If that boy does not have diversion or friends or companions in his games, his life will be like a narrow prison in which he sees nothing but spiderwebs and hears nothing but the crawling of insects.

That sorrow which obsessed me during my youth was not caused by lack of amusement, because I could have had it; neither from lack of friends, because I could have found them. That sorrow was caused by an inward ailment which made me love solitude. It killed in me the inclination for games and amusement. It removed from my shoulders the wings of youth and made me like a pond of water between mountains which reflects in its calm surface the shadows of ghosts and the colors of clouds and trees, but cannot find an outlet by which to pass singing to the sea.

Thus was my life before I attained the age of eighteen. That year is like a mountain peak in my life, for it awakened knowledge in me and made me understand the vicissitudes of mankind. In that year I was reborn and unless a person is born again his life will remain like a blank sheet in the book of existence. In that year, I saw the angels of Heaven looking at me through the eyes of a beautiful woman. I also saw the devils of hell raging in the heart of an evil man. He who does not see the angels and devils in the beauty and malice of life will be far removed from knowledge, and his spirit will be empty of affection.

THE HAND OF DESTINY

N THE SPRING OF
that wonderful year, I was in Beirut. The gardens
were full of Nisan flowers and the earth was carpeted with green grass, all like a secret of earth revealed to Heaven. The orange trees and apple trees,
looking like houris or brides sent by nature to inspire
poets and excite the imagination, were wearing white
garments of perfumed blossoms.

Spring is beautiful everywhere, but it is most
beautiful in Lebanon. It is a spirit that roams round
the earth but hovers over Lebanon, conversing with

kings and prophets, singing with the rivers the songs of Solomon, and repeating with the Holy Cedars of Lebanon the memory of ancient glory. Beirut, free from the mud of winter and the dust of summer, is like a bride in the spring, or like a mermaid sitting by the side of a brook drying her smooth skin in the rays of the sun.

One day, in the month of Nisan, I went to visit a friend whose home was at some distance from the glamorous city. As we were conversing, a dignified man of about sixty-five entered the house. As I rose to greet him, my friend introduced him to me as Farris Effandi Karamy and then gave him my name with flattering words. The old man looked at me a moment, touching his forehead with the ends of his fingers as if he were trying to regain his memory. Then he smilingly approached me, saying, "You are the son of a very dear friend of mine, and I am happy to see that friend in your person."

Much affected by his words, I was attracted to him like a bird whose instinct leads him to his nest before the coming of the tempest. As we sat down, he told us about his friendship with my father, recalling the time which they spent together. An old man likes to return in memory to the days of his youth like a stranger who longs to go back to his own country. He delights to tell stories of the past like a

24

poet who takes pleasure in reciting his best poem. He lives spiritually in the past because the present passes swiftly, and the future seems to him an approach to the oblivion of the grave. An hour full of old memories passed like the shadows of the trees over the grass. When Farris Effandi started to leave, he put his left hand on my shoulder and shook my right hand, saying, "I have not seen your father for twenty years. I hope you will take his place in frequent visits to my house." I promised gratefully to do my duty toward a dear friend of my father.

When the old man left the house, I asked my friend to tell me more about him. He said, "I do not know any other man in Beirut whose wealth has made him kind and whose kindness has made him wealthy. He is one of the few who come to this world and leave it without harming any one, but people of that kind are usually miserable and oppressed because they are not clever enough to save themselves from the crookedness of others. Farris Effandi has one daughter whose character is similar to his and whose beauty and gracefulness are beyond description, and she will also be miserable because her father's wealth is placing her already at the edge of a horrible precipice."

As he uttered these words, I noticed that his face clouded. Then he continued, "Farris Effandi is a

25

good old man with a noble heart, but he lacks will power. People lead him like a blind man. His daughter obeys him in spite of her pride and intelligence, and this is the secret which lurks in the life of father and daughter. This secret was discovered by an evil man who is a bishop and whose wickedness hides in the shadow of his Gospel. He makes the people believe that he is kind and noble. He is the head of religion in this land of the religious. The people obey and worship him. He leads them like a flock of lambs to the slaughter house. This bishop has a nephew who is full of hatefulness and corruption. The day will come sooner or later when he will place his nephew on his right and Farris Effandi's daughter on his left, and, holding with his evil hand the wreath of matrimony over their heads, will tie a pure virgin to a filthy degenerate, placing the heart of the day in the bosom of night.

"That is all I can tell you about Farris Effandi and his daughter, so do not ask me any more questions."

Saying this, he turned his head toward the window as if he were trying to solve the problems of human existence by concentrating on the beauty of the universe.

As I left the house, I told my friend that I was going to visit Farris Effandi in a few days for the

26

purpose of fulfilling my promise and for the sake of the friendship which had joined him and my father. He stared at me for a moment, and I noticed a change in his expression as if my few simple words had revealed to him a new idea. Then he looked straight through my eyes in a strange manner, a look of love, mercy, and fear—the look of a prophet who foresees what no one else can divine. Then his lips trembled a little, but he said nothing when I started toward the door. That strange look followed me, the meaning of which I could not understand until I grew up in the world of experience, where hearts understand each other intuitively and where spirits are mature with knowledge.

3

ENTRANCE TO THE SHRINE

N A FEW DAYS,
loneliness overcame me; and I tired of the grim faces
of books; I hired a carriage and started for the house
of Farris Effandi. As I reached the pine woods where
people went for picnics, the driver took a private
way, shaded with willow trees on each side. Passing
through, we could see the beauty of the green grass,
the grapevines, and the many colored flowers of
Nisan just blossoming.

In a few minutes the carriage stopped before a
solitary house in the midst of a beautiful garden. The

scent of roses, gardenia, and jasmine filled the air. As I dismounted and entered the spacious garden, I saw Farris Effandi coming to meet me. He ushered me into his house with a hearty welcome and sat by me, like a happy father when he sees his son, showering me with questions on my life, future and education. I answered him, my voice full of ambition and zeal; for I heard ringing in my ears the hymn of glory, and I was sailing the calm sea of hopeful dreams. Just then a beautiful young woman, dressed in a gorgeous white silk gown, appeared from behind the velvet curtains of the door and walked toward me. Farris Effandi and I rose from our seats.

"This is my daughter Selma," said the old man. Then he introduced me to her, saying, "Fate has brought back to me a dear old friend of mine in the person of his son." Selma stared at me a moment as if doubting that a visitor could have entered their house. Her hand, when I touched it, was like a white lily, and a strange pang pierced my heart.

We all sat silent as if Selma had brought into the room with her a heavenly spirit worthy of mute respect. As she felt the silence she smiled at me and said, "Many a time my father has repeated to me the stories of his youth and of the old days he and your father spent together If your father spoke to you in the same way, then this meeting is not the first one between us."

The old man was delighted to hear his daughter talking in such a manner and said, "Selma is very sentimental. She sees everything through the eyes of the spirit." Then he resumed his conversation with care and tact as if he had found in me a magic charm which took him on the wings of memory to the days of the past.

As I considered him, dreaming of my own later years, he looked upon me, as a lofty old tree that has withstood storms and sunshine throws its shadow upon a small sapling which shakes before the breeze of dawn.

But Selma was silent. Occasionally, she looked first at me and then at her father as if reading the first and last chapters of life's drama. The day passed fast in that garden, and I could see through the window the ghostly yellow kiss of sunset on the mountains of Lebanon. Farris Effandi continued to recount his experiences and I listened entranced and responded with such enthusiasm that his sorrow was changed to happiness.

Selma sat by the window, looking on with sorrowful eyes and not speaking, although beauty has its own heavenly language, loftier than the voices of tongues and lips. It is a timeless language, common to all humanity, a calm lake that attracts the singing rivulets to its depth and makes them silent.

Only our spirits can understand beauty, or live and grow with it. It puzzles our minds; we are unable to describe it in words; it is a sensation that our eyes cannot see, derived from both the one who observes and the one who is looked upon. Real beauty is a ray which emanates from the holy of holies of the spirit, and illuminates the body, as life comes from the depths of the earth and gives color and scent to a flower.

Real beauty lies in the spiritual accord that is called love which can exist between a man and a woman.

Did my spirit and Selma's reach out to each other that day when we met, and did that yearning make me see her as the most beautiful woman under the sun? Or was I intoxicated with the wine of youth which made me fancy that which never existed?

Did my youth blind my natural eyes and make me imagine the brightness of her eyes, the sweetness of her mouth, and the grace of her figure? Or was it that her brightness, sweetness, and grace opened my eyes and showed me the happiness and sorrow of love?

34

It is hard to answer these questions, but I say truly that in that hour I felt an emotion that I had never felt before, a new affection resting calmly in my heart, like the spirit hovering over the waters at the creation of the world, and from that affection was born my happiness and my sorrow. Thus ended the hour of my first meeting with Selma, and thus the will of Heaven freed me from the bondage of youth and solitude and let me walk in the procession of love.

Love is the only freedom in the world because it so elevates the spirit that the laws of humanity and the phenomena of nature do not alter its course.

As I rose from my seat to depart, Farris Effandi came close to me and said soberly, "Now my son, since you know your way to this house, you should come often and feel that you are coming to your father's house. Consider me as a father and Selma as a sister." Saying this, he turned to Selma as if to ask confirmation of his statement. She nodded her head positively and then looked at me as one who has found an old acquaintance.

Those words uttered by Farris Effandi Karamy placed me side by side with his daughter at the altar of love. Those words were a heavenly song which started with exaltation and ended with sorrow; they raised our spirits to the realm of light and searing flame; they were the cup from which we drank happiness and bitterness.

I left the house. The old man accompanied me to the edge of the garden, while my heart throbbed like the trembling lips of a thirsty man.

THE WHITE TORCH

HE MONTH OF NISAN had nearly passed. I continued to visit the home of Farris Effendi and to meet Selma in that beautiful garden, gazing upon her beauty, marveling at her intelligence, and hearing the stillness of sorrow. I felt an invisible hand drawing me to her.

Every visit gave me a new meaning to her beauty and a new insight into her sweet spirit, until she became a book whose pages I could understand and whose praises I could sing, but which I could never finish reading. A woman whom Providence has pro-

39

vided with beauty of spirit and body is a truth, at the same time both open and secret, which we can understand only by love, and touch only by virtue; and when we attempt to describe such a woman she disappears like a vapor.

Selma Karamy had bodily and spiritual beauty, but how can I describe her to one who never knew her? Can a dead man remember the singing of a nightingale and the fragrance of a rose and the sigh of a brook? Can a prisoner who is heavily loaded with shackles follow the breeze of the dawn? Is not silence more painful than death? Does pride prevent me from describing Selma in plain words since I cannot draw her truthfully with luminous colors? A hungry man in a desert will not refuse to eat dry bread if Heaven does not shower him with manna and quails.

In her white silk dress, Selma was slender as a ray of moonlight coming through the window. She walked gracefully and rhythmically. Her voice was low and sweet; words fell from her lips like drops of dew falling from the petals of flowers when they are disturbed by the wind.

But Selma's face! No words can describe its expression, reflecting first great internal suffering, then heavenly exaltation.

The beauty of Selma's face was not classic; it

was like a dream of revelation which cannot be measured or bound or copied by the brush of a painter, or the chisel of a sculptor. Selma's beauty was not in her golden hair, but in the virtue and purity which surrounded it; not in her large eyes, but in the light which emanated from them; not in her red lips, but in the sweetness of her words; not in her ivory neck, but in its slight bow to the front. Nor was it in her perfect figure, but in the nobility of her spirit, burning like a white torch between earth and sky. Her beauty was like a gift of poetry. But poets are unhappy people, for, no matter how high their spirits reach, they will still be enclosed in an envelope of tears.

Selma was deeply thoughtful rather than talkative, and her silence was a kind of music that carried one to a world of dreams and made him listen to the throbbing of his heart, and see the ghosts of his thoughts and feelings standing before him, looking him in the eyes.

She wore a cloak of deep sorrow through her life, which increased her strange beauty and dignity, as a tree in blossom is more lovely when seen through the mist of dawn.

Sorrow linked her spirit and mine, as if each saw in the other's face what the heart was feeling and heard the echo of a hidden voice. God had made two bodies in one, and separation could be nothing but agony.

The sorrowful spirit finds rest when united with a similar one. They join affectionately, as a stranger is cheered when he sees another stranger in a strange land. Hearts that are united through the medium of sorrow will not be separated by the glory of happiness. Love that is cleansed by tears will remain eternally pure and beautiful.

THE TEMPEST

 NE DAY FARRIS
Effandi invited me to dinner at his home. I accepted,
my spirit hungry for the divine bread which Heaven
placed in the hands of Selma, the spiritual bread
which makes our hearts hungrier the more we eat of
it. It was this bread which Kais, the Arabian poet,
Dante, and Sappho tasted and which set their hearts
afire; the bread which the Goddess prepares with the
sweetness of kisses and the bitterness of tears.

As I reached the home of Farris Effandi, I saw
Selma sitting on a bench in the garden resting her

45

head against a tree and looking like a bride in her white silk dress, or like a sentinel guarding that place.

Silently and reverently I approached and sat by her. I could not talk; so I resorted to silence, the only language of the heart, but I felt that Selma was listening to my wordless call and watching the ghost of my soul in my eyes.

In a few minutes the old man came out and greeted me as usual. When he stretched his hand toward me, I felt as if he were blessing the secrets that united me and his daughter. Then he said, "Dinner is ready, my children; let us eat." We rose and followed him, and Selma's eyes brightened; for a new sentiment had been added to her love by her father's calling us his children.

We sat at the table enjoying the food and sipping the old wine, but our souls were living in a world far away. We were dreaming of the future and its hardships.

Three persons were separated in thoughts, but united in love; three innocent people with much feeling but little knowledge; a drama was being performed by an old man who loved his daughter and cared for her happiness, a young woman of twenty looking into the future with anxiety, and a young man, dreaming and worrying, who had tasted neither the wine of life nor its vinegar, and trying to reach the height of love and knowledge but unable to lift himself up. We three sitting in twilight were eating and drinking in that solitary home, guarded by Heaven's eyes, but at the bottoms of our glasses were hidden bitterness and anguish.

As we finished eating, one of the maids announced the presence of a man at the door who wished to see Farris Effandi. "Who is he?" asked the old man. "The Bishop's messenger," said the maid. There was a moment of silence during which Farris Effandi stared at his daughter like a prophet who gazes at Heaven to divine its secret. Then he said to the maid, "Let the man in."

As the maid left, a man, dressed in oriental uniform and with a big mustache curled at the ends, entered and greeted the old man, saying, "His Grace, the Bishop, has sent me for you with his private carriage; he wishes to discuss important business with you." The old man's face clouded and his smile disappeared. After a moment of deep thought he came close to me and said in a friendly voice, "I hope to find you here when I come back, for Selma will enjoy your company in this solitary place."

Saying this, he turned to Selma and, smiling, asked her if she agreed. She nodded her head, but her cheeks became red, and with a voice sweeter than the music of a lyre she said, "I will do my best, Father, to make our guest happy."

Selma watched the carriage that had taken her father and the Bishop's messenger until it disappeared. Then she came and sat opposite me on a divan covered with green silk. She looked like a lily bent to the carpet of green grass by the breeze of dawn. It was the will of Heaven that I should be with Selma alone, at night, in her beautiful home surrounded by trees, where silence, love, beauty, and virtue dwelt together.

We were both silent, each waiting for the other to speak, but speech is not the only means of understanding between two souls. It is not the syllables that come from the lips and tongues that bring hearts together.

There is something greater and purer than what the mouth utters. Silence illuminates our souls, whispers to our hearts, and brings them together. Silence separates us from ourselves, makes us sail the firmament of spirit, and brings us closer to Heaven; it makes us feel that bodies are no more than prisons and that this world is only a place of exile.

Selma looked at me and her eyes revealed the secret of her heart. Then she quietly said, "Let us go to the garden and sit under the trees and watch the

48

moon come up behind the mountains." Obediently I rose from my seat, but I hesitated.

"Don't you think we had better stay here until the moon has risen and illuminates the garden?" And I continued, "The darkness hides the trees and flowers. We can see nothing."

Then she said, "If darkness hides the trees and flowers from our eyes, it will not hide love from our hearts."

Uttering these words in a strange tone, she turned her eyes and looked through the window. I remained silent, pondering her words, weighing the true meaning of each syllable. Then she looked at me as if she regretted what she had said and tried to take away those words from my ears by the magic of her eyes. But those eyes, instead of making me forget what she had said, repeated through the depths of my heart more clearly and effectively the sweet words which had already become graven in my memory for eternity.

Every beauty and greatness in this world is created by a single thought or emotion inside a man. Every thing we see today, made by past generations, was, before its appearance, a thought in the mind of a man or an impulse in the heart of a woman. The revolutions that shed so much blood and turned men's minds toward liberty were the idea of one man who lived in the midst of thousands of men. The devastating wars which destroyed empires were a thought that existed in the mind of an individual. The supreme teachings that changed the course of humanity were the ideas of a man whose genius separated him from his environment. A single thought built the Pyramids, founded the glory of Islam, and caused the burning of the library at Alexandria.

One thought will come to you at night which will elevate you to glory or lead you to the asylum. One look from a woman's eye makes you the happiest man in the world. One word from a man's lips will make you rich or poor.

That word which Selma uttered that night arrested me between my past and future, as a boat which is anchored in the midst of the ocean. That word awakened me from the slumber of youth and solitude and set me on the stage where life and death play their parts.

The scent of flowers mingled with the breeze as we came into the garden and sat silently on a bench near a jasmine tree, listening to the breathing of sleeping nature, while in the blue sky the eyes of heaven witnessed our drama.

The moon came out from behind Mount Sunnin

and shone over the coast, hills, and mountains; and we could see the villages fringing the valley like apparitions which have suddenly been conjured from nothing. We could see the beauty of all Lebanon under the silver rays of the moon.

Poets of the West think of Lebanon as a legendary place, forgotten since the passing of David and Solomon and the Prophets, as the Garden of Eden became lost after the fall of Adam and Eve. To those Western Poets, the word "Lebanon" is a poetical expression associated with a mountain whose sides are drenched with the incense of the Holy Cedars. It reminds them of the temples of copper and marble standing stern and impregnable and of a herd of deer feeding in the valleys. That night I saw Lebanon dream-like with the eyes of a poet.

Thus, the appearance of things changes according to the emotions, and thus we see magic and beauty in them, while the magic and beauty are really in ourselves.

As the rays of the moon shone on the face, neck, and arms of Selma, she looked like a statue of ivory sculptured by the fingers of some worshiper of Ishtar, goddess of beauty and love. As she looked at me, she said, "Why are you silent? Why do you not tell me something about your past?" As I gazed at her, my muteness vanished, and I opened my lips and said, "Did you not hear what I said when we came to this orchard? The spirit that hears the whispering of flowers and the singing of silence can also hear the shrieking of my soul and the clamor of my heart."

She covered her face with her hands and said in a trembling voice, "Yes, I heard you—I heard a voice coming from the bosom of night and a clamor raging in the heart of the day."

Forgetting my past, my very existence—everything but Selma—I answered her, saying, "And I heard you, too, Selma. I heard exhilarating music pulsing in the air and causing the whole universe to tremble."

Upon hearing these words, she closed her eyes and on her lips I saw a smile of pleasure mingled with sadness. She whispered softly, "Now I know that there is something higher than heaven and deeper than the ocean and stranger than life and death and time. I know now what I did not know before."

At that moment Selma became dearer than a friend and closer than a sister and more beloved than a sweetheart. She became a supreme thought, a beautiful dream, an overpowering emotion living in my spirit.

It is wrong to think that love comes from long

companionship and persevering courtship. Love is the offspring of spiritual affinity and unless that affinity is created in a moment, it will not be created in years or even generations.

Then Selma raised her head and gazed at the horizon where Mount Sunnin meets the sky, and said, "Yesterday you were like a brother to me, with whom I lived and by whom I sat calmly under my father's care. Now, I feel the presence of something stranger and sweeter than brotherly affection, an unfamiliar commingling of love and fear that fills my heart with sorrow and happiness."

I responded, "This emotion which we fear and which shakes us when it passes through our hearts is the law of nature that guides the moon around the earth and the sun around God."

She put her hand on my head and wove her fingers through my hair. Her face brightened and tears came out of her eyes like drops of dew on the leaves of a lily, and she said, "Who would believe our story—who would believe that in this hour we have surmounted the obstacles of doubt? Who would believe that the month of Nisan which brought us together for the first time, is the month that halted us in the Holy of Holies of life?"

Her hand was still on my head as she spoke, and

I would not have preferred a royal crown or a wreath of glory to that beautiful smooth hand whose fingers were twined in my hair.

Then I answered her: "People will not believe our story because they do not know that love is the only flower that grows and blossoms without the aid of seasons, but was it Nisan that brought us together for the first time, and is it this hour that has arrested us in the Holy of Holies of life? Is it not the hand of God that brought our souls close together before birth and made us prisoners of each other for all the days and nights? Man's life does not commence in the womb and never ends in the grave; and this firmament, full of moonlight and stars, is not deserted by loving souls and intuitive spirits."

As she drew her hand away from my head, I felt a kind of electrical vibration at the roots of my hair mingled with the night breeze. Like a devoted worshiper who receives his blessing by kissing the altar in a shrine, I took Selma's hand, placed my burning lips on it, and gave it a long kiss, the memory of which melts my heart and awakens by its sweetness all the virtue of my spirit.

An hour passed, every minute of which was a year of love. The silence of the night, moonlight, flowers, and trees made us forget all reality except love, when suddenly we heard the galloping of horses and rattling of carriage wheels. Awakened from our pleasant swoon and plunged from the world of dreams into the world of perplexity and misery, we found that the old man had returned from his mission. We rose and walked through the orchard to meet him.

When the carriage reached the entrance of the garden, Farris Effandi dismounted and slowly walked towards us, bending forward slightly as if he were carrying a heavy load. He approached Selma and placed both of his hands on her shoulders and stared at her. Tears coursed down his wrinkled cheeks and his lips trembled with sorrowful smile. In a choking voice, he said, "My beloved Selma, very soon you will be taken away from the arms of your father to the arms of another man. Very soon fate will carry you from this lonely home to the world's spacious court, and this garden will miss the pressure of your footsteps, and your father will become a stranger to you. All is done; may God bless you."

Hearing these words, Selma's face clouded and her eyes froze as if she felt a premonition of death. Then she screamed, like a bird shot down, suffering, and trembling, and in a choked voice said, "What do you say? What do you mean? Where are you sending me?"

Then she looked at him searchingly, trying to discover his secret. In a moment she said, "I understand.

I understand everything. The Bishop has demanded me from you and has prepared a cage for this bird with broken wings. Is this your will, Father?"

His answer was a deep sigh. Tenderly he led Selma into the house while I remained standing in the garden, waves of perplexity beating upon me like a tempest upon autumn leaves. Then I followed them into the living room, and to avoid embarrassment, shook the old man's hand, looked at Selma, my beautiful star, and left the house.

As I reached the end of the garden I heard the old man calling me and turned to meet him. Apologetically he took my hand and said, "Forgive me, my son. I have ruined your evening with the shedding of tears, but please come to see me when my house is deserted and I am lonely and desperate. Youth, my dear son, does not combine with senility, as morning does not meet the night; but you will come to me and call to my memory the youthful days which I spent with your father, and you will tell me the news of life which does not count me as among its sons any longer. Will you not visit me when Selma leaves and I am left here in loneliness?"

While he said these sorrowful words and I silently shook his hand, I felt the warm tears falling from his eyes upon my hand. Trembling with sorrow and filial affection, I felt as if my heart were choked with

56

grief. When I raised my head and he saw the tears in my eyes, he bent toward me and touched my forehead with his lips. "Good-bye, son, Good-bye."

An old man's tear is more potent than that of a young man because it is the residuum of life in his weakening body. A young man's tear is like a drop of dew on the leaf of a rose, while that of an old man is like a yellow leaf which falls with the wind at the approach of winter.

As I left the house of Farris Effandi Karamy, Selma's voice still rang in my ears, her beauty followed me like a wraith, and her father's tears dried slowly on my hand.

My departure was like Adam's exodus from Paradise, but the Eve of my heart was not with me to make the whole world an Eden. That night, in which I had been born again, I felt that I saw death's face for the first time.

Thus the sun enlivens and kills the fields with its heat.

6

THE LAKE OF FIRE

 VERYTHING THAT
a man does secretly in the darkness of night will be
clearly revealed in daylight. Words uttered in pri-
vacy will become unexpectedly common conversation. Deeds which we hide today in the corners of
our lodgings will be shouted on every street tomorrow.

Thus the ghosts of darkness revealed the purpose
of Bishop Bulos Galib's meeting with Farris Effandi
Karamy, and his conversation was repeated all over
the neighborhood until it reached my ears.

The discussion that took place between Bishop Bulos Galib and Farris Effandi that night was not over the problems of the poor or the widows and orphans. The main purpose for sending after Farris Effandi and bringing him in the Bishop's private carriage was the betrothal of Selma to the Bishop's nephew, Mansour Bey Galib.

Selma was the only child of the wealthy Farris Effandi, and the Bishop's choice fell on Selma, not on account of her beauty and noble spirit, but on account of her father's money which would guarantee Mansour Bey a good and prosperous fortune and make him an important man.

The heads of religion in the East are not satisfied with their own munificence, but they must strive to make all members of their families superiors and oppressors. The glory of a prince goes to his eldest son by inheritance, but the exaltation of a religious head is contagious among his brothers and nephews. Thus the Christian bishop and the Moslem imam and the Brahman priest become like sea reptiles who clutch their prey with many tentacles and suck their blood with numerous mouths.

When the Bishop demanded Selma's hand for his nephew, the only answer that he received from her father was deep silence and falling tears, for he hated to lose his only child. Any man's soul trembles when he is separated from his only daughter whom he has reared to young womanhood.

The sorrow of parents at the marriage of a daughter is equal to their happiness at the marriage of a son, because a son brings to the family a new member, while a daughter, upon her marriage, is lost to them.

Farris Effandi perforce granted the Bishop's request, obeying his will unwillingly, because Farris Effandi knew the Bishop's nephew very well, knew that he was dangerous, full of hate, wickedness, and corruption.

In Lebanon, no Christian could oppose his bishop and remain in good standing. No man could disobey his religious head and keep his reputation. The eye could not resist a spear without being pierced, and the hand could not grasp a sword without being cut off.

Suppose that Farris Effandi had resisted the Bishop and refused his wish; then Selma's reputation would have been ruined and her name would have been blemished by the dirt of lips and tongues. In the opinion of the fox, high bunches of grapes that can't be reached are sour.

Thus destiny seized Selma and led her like a humiliated slave in the procession of miserable oriental woman, and thus fell that noble spirit into the trap after having flown freely on the white wings of love in a sky full of moonlight scented with the odor of flowers.

In some countries, the parent's wealth is a source of misery for the children. The wide strong box which the father and mother together have used for the safety of their wealth becomes a narrow, dark prison for the souls of their heirs. The Almighty Dinar* which the people worship becomes a demon which punishes the spirit and deadens the heart. Selma Karamy was one of those who were victims of their parents' wealth and bridegrooms' cupidity. Had it not been for her father's wealth, Selma would still be living happily.

A week had passed. The love of Selma was my sole entertainer, singing songs of happiness for me at night and waking me at dawn to reveal the meaning of life and the secrets of nature. It is a heavenly love that is free from jealousy, rich and never harmful to the spirit. It is a deep affinity that bathes the soul in contentment; a deep hunger for affection which, when satisfied, fills the soul with bounty; a tenderness that creates hope without agitating the soul, changing earth to paradise and life to a sweet and beautiful dream. In the morning, when I walked in the fields, I saw the token of Eternity in the awakening of

* Kind of money used in the Near East.

nature, and when I sat by the seashore I heard the waves singing the song of Eternity. And when I walked in the streets I saw the beauty of life and the splendor of humanity in the appearance of passers-by and movements of workers.

Those days passed like ghosts and disappeared like clouds, and soon nothing was left for me but sorrowful memories. The eyes with which I used to look at the beauty of spring and the awakening of nature, could see nothing but the fury of the tempest and the misery of winter. The ears with which I formerly heard with delight the song of the waves, could hear only the howling of the wind and the wrath of the sea against the precipice. The soul which had observed happily the tireless vigor of mankind and the glory of the universe, was tortured by the knowledge of disappointment and failure. Nothing was more beautiful than those days of love, and nothing was more bitter than those horrible nights of sorrow.

When I could no longer resist the impulse, I went, on the weekend, once more to Selma's home—the shrine which Beauty had erected and which Love had blessed, in which the spirit could worship and the heart kneel humbly and pray. When I entered the garden I felt a power pulling me away from this world and placing me in a sphere supernaturally free from struggle and hardship. Like a mystic who receives a revelation of Heaven, I saw myself amid the trees and flowers, and as I approached the entrance of the house I beheld Selma sitting on the bench in the shadow of a jasmine tree where we both had sat the week before, on that night which Providence had chosen for the beginning of my happiness and sorrow.

She neither moved nor spoke as I approached her. She seemed to have known intuitively that I was coming, and when I sat by her she gazed at me for a moment and sighed deeply, then turned her head and looked at the sky. And, after a moment full of magic silence, she turned back toward me and tremblingly took my hand and said in a faint voice, "Look at me, my friend; study my face and read in it that which you want to know and which I can not recite. Look at me, my beloved . . . look at me, my brother."

I gazed at her intently and saw that those eyes, which a few days ago were smiling like lips and moving like the wings of a nightingale, were already sunken and glazed with sorrow and pain. Her face, that had resembled the unfolding, sunkissed leaves of a lily, had faded and become colorless. Her sweet lips were like two withering roses that autumn has left on their stems. Her neck, that had been a column

66

of ivory, was bent forward as if it no longer could support the burden of grief in her head.

All these changes I saw in Selma's face, but to me they were like a passing cloud that covered the face of the moon and makes it more beautiful. A look which reveals inward stress adds more beauty to the face, no matter how much tragedy and pain it bespeaks; but the face which, in silence, does not announce hidden mysteries is not beautiful, regardless of the symmetry of its features. The cup does not entice our lips unless the wine's color is seen through the transparent crystal.

Selma, on that evening, was like a cup full of heavenly wine concocted of the bitterness and sweetness of life. Unaware, she symbolized the oriental woman who never leaves her parents' home until she puts upon her neck the heavy yoke of her husband, who never leaves her loving mother's arms until she must live as a slave, enduring the harshness of her husband's mother.

I continued to look at Selma and listen to her depressed spirit and suffer with her until I felt that time had ceased and the universe had faded from existence. I could see only her two large eyes staring fixedly at me and could feel only her cold, trembling hand holding mine.

I woke from my swoon hearing Selma saying

quietly, "Come, my beloved, let us discuss the horrible future before it comes. My father has just left the house to see the man who is going to be my companion until death. My father, whom God chose for the purpose of my existence, will meet the man whom the world has selected to be my master for the rest of my life. In the heart of this city, the old man who accompanied me during my youth will meet the young man who will be my companion for the coming years. Tonight the two families will set the marriage date. What a strange and impressive hour! Last week at this time, under this jasmine tree, Love embraced my soul for the first time, while Destiny was writing the first word of my life's story at the Bishop's mansion. Now, while my father and my suitor are planning the day of marriage, I see your spirit quivering around me as a thirsty bird flickers above a spring of water guarded by a hungry serpent. Oh, how great this night is! And how deep is its mystery!"

Hearing these words, I felt that the dark ghost of complete despondency was seizing our love to choke it in its infancy, and I answered her, "That bird will remain flickering over that spring until thirst destroys him or falls into the grasp of a serpent and becomes its prey."

She responded, "No, my beloved, this nightingale should remain alive and sing until dark comes, until spring passes, until the end of the world, and keep on singing eternally. His voice should not be silenced, because he brings life to my heart, his wings should not be broken, because their motion removes the cloud from my heart."

Then I whispered, "Selma, my beloved, thirst will exhaust him; and fear will kill him."

She replied immediately with trembling lips, "The thirst of soul is sweeter than the wine of material things, and the fear of spirit is dearer than the security of the body. But listen, my beloved, listen carefully, I am standing today at the door of a new life which I know nothing about. I am like a blind man who feels his way so that he will not fall. My father's wealth has placed me in the slave market, and this man has bought me. I neither know nor love him but I shall learn to love him, and I shall obey him, serve him, and make him happy. I shall give him all that a weak woman can give a strong man.

"But you, my beloved, are still in the prime of life. You can walk freely upon life's spacious path, carpeted with flowers. You are free to traverse the world, making of your heart a torch to light your way. You can think, talk, and act freely; you can write your name on the face of life because you are a man; you can live as a master because your father's wealth will not place you in the slave market to be bought and sold; you can marry the woman of your choice and, before she lives in your home, you can let her reside in your heart and can exchange confidences without hindrance."

Silence prevailed for a moment, and Selma continued, "But, is it now that Life will tear us apart so that you may attain the glory of a man and I the duty of a woman? Is it for this that the valley swallows the song of the nightingale in its depths, and the wind scatters the petals of the rose, and the feet tread upon the wine cup? Were all those nights we spent in the moonlight by the jasmine tree, where our souls united, in vain? Did we fly swiftly toward the stars until our wings tired, and are we descending now into the abyss? Or was Love asleep when he came to us, and did he, when he woke, become angry and decide to punish us? Or did our spirits turn the night's breeze into a wind that tore us to pieces and blew us like dust to the depth of the valley? We disobeyed no commandment, nor did we taste of forbidden fruit, so what is making us leave this paradise? We never conspired or practised mutiny, then why are we descending to hell? No, no, the moments which united us are greater than centuries, and the light that illuminated our spirits is stronger than the dark; and if the tempest separates us on this rough ocean, the waves will unite us on the calm shore; and if this life kills us, death will unite us. A woman's heart will not change with time or season; even if it dies eternally, it will never perish. A woman's heart is like a field turned into a battleground; after the trees are uprooted and the grass is burned and the rocks are reddened with blood and the earth is planted with bones and skulls, it is calm and silent as if nothing has happened; for the spring and autumn come at their intervals and resume their work.

"And now, my beloved, what shall we do? How shall we part and when shall we meet? Shall we consider love a strange visitor who came in the evening and left us in the morning? Or shall we suppose this affection a dream that came in our sleep and departed when we awoke?

"Shall we consider this week an hour of intoxication to be replaced by soberness? Raise your head and let me look at you, my beloved; open your lips and let me hear your voice. Speak to me! Will you remember me after this tempest has sunk the ship of our love? Will you hear the whispering of my wings in the silence of the night? Will you hear my spirit fluttering over you? Will you listen to my sighs? Will you see my shadow approach with the shadows of dusk and disappear with the flush of dawn? Tell me, my beloved, what will you be after having been magic ray to my eyes, sweet song to my ears, and wings to my soul? What will you be?"

Hearing these words, my heart melted, and I answered her, "I will be as you want me to be, my beloved."

Then she said, "I want you to love me as a poet loves his sorrowful thoughts. I want you to remember me as a traveler remembers a calm pool in which his image was reflected as he drank its water. I want you to remember me as a mother remembers her child that died before it saw the light, and I want you to remember me as a merciful king remembers a prisoner who died before his pardon reached him. I want you to be my companion, and I want you to visit my father and console him in his solitude because I shall be leaving him soon and shall be a stranger to him."

I answered her, saying, "I will do all you have said and will make my soul an envelope for your soul, and my heart a residence for your beauty and my breast a grave for your sorrows. I shall love you, Selma, as the prairies love the spring, and I shall live in you the life of a flower under the sun's rays. I shall sing your name as the valley sings the echo of the bells of the village churches; I shall listen to the language of your soul as the shore listens to the story of the waves. I shall remember you as a stranger remembers his beloved country, and as a hungry man remembers a banquet, and as a dethroned king remembers the days of his glory, and as a prisoner remembers the hours of ease and freedom. I shall remember you as a sower remembers the bundles of wheat on his threshing floor, and as a shepherd remembers the green prairies and sweet brooks."

Selma listened to my words with palpitating heart, and said, "Tomorrow the truth will become ghostly and the awakening will be like a dream. Will a lover be satisfied embracing a ghost, or will a thirsty man quench his thirst from the spring of a dream?"

I answered her, "Tomorrow, destiny will put you in the midst of a peaceful family, but it will send me into the world of struggle and warfare. You will be in the home of a person whom chance has made most fortunate through your beauty and virtue, while I shall be living a life of suffering and fear. You will enter the gate of life, while I shall enter the gate of death. You will be received hospitably, while I shall exist in solitude, but I shall erect a statue of love and worship it in the valley of death. Love will be my sole comforter, and I shall drink love like wine and wear it like a garment. At dawn, Love will wake me from slumber and take me to the distant field, and at noon will lead me to the shadows of trees, where I will find shelter with the birds from the heat of the sun. In the evening, it will cause me to pause before sunset to hear nature's farewell song to the light of day and will show me ghostly clouds sailing in the sky. At night, Love will embrace me, and I shall sleep, dreaming of the heavenly world where the spirits of lovers and poets abide. In the Spring I shall walk side by side with love among violets and jasmines and drink the remaining drops of winter in the lily cups. In Summer we shall make the bundles of hay our pillows and the grass our bed, and the blue sky will cover us as we gaze at the stars and moon.

"In Autumn, Love and I will go to the vineyard and sit by the wine press and watch the grapevines being denuded of their golden ornaments, and the migrating flocks of birds will wing over us. In Winter we shall sit by the fireside reciting stories of long ago and chronicles of far countries. During my youth, Love will be my teacher; in middle age, my help; and in old age, my delight. Love, my beloved Selma, will stay with me to the end of my life, and after death the hand of God will unite us again."

All these words came from the depths of my heart like flames of fire which leap raging from the hearth and then disappear in the ashes. Selma was weeping as if her eyes were lips answering me with tears.

Those whom love has not given wings cannot fly behind the cloud of appearances to see the magic world in which Selma's spirit and mine existed together in that sorrowfully happy hour. Those whom Love has not chosen as followers do not hear when Love calls. This story is not for them. Even if they should comprehend these pages, they would not be able to grasp the shadowy meanings which are not clothed in words and do not reside on paper, but what human being is he who has never sipped the wine from the cup of love, and what spirit is it that has never stood reverently before that lighted altar in the temple whose pavement is the hearts of men and women and whose ceiling is the secret canopy of dreams? What flower is that on whose leaves the dawn has never poured a drop of dew; what streamlet is that which lost its course without going to the sea?

Selma raised her face toward the sky and gazed at the heavenly stars which studded the firmament. She stretched out her hands; her eyes widened, and her lips trembled. On her pale face, I could see the signs of sorrow, oppression, hopelessness, and pain. Then she cried, "Oh, Lord, what has a woman done that hath offended Thee? What sin has she committed to deserve such a punishment? For what crime has she been awarded everlasting castigation? Oh, Lord, Thou art strong, and I am weak. Why hast Thou made me suffer pain? Thou art great and almighty,

75

while I am nothing but a tiny creature crawling before Thy throne. Why hast Thou crushed me with Thy foot? Thou art a raging tempest, and I am like dust; why, my Lord, hast Thou flung me upon the cold earth? Thou art powerful, and I am helpless; why art Thou fighting me? Thou art considerate, and I am prudent; why art Thou destroying me? Thou hast created woman with love, and why, with love, dost Thou ruin her? With Thy right hand dost Thou lift her, and with Thy left hand dost Thou strike her into the abyss, and she knows not why. In her mouth Thou blowest the breath of life, and in her heart Thou sowest the seeds of death. Thou dost show her the path of happiness, but Thou leadest her in the road of misery; in her mouth Thou dost place a song of happiness, but then Thou dost close her lips with sorrow and dost fetter her tongue with agony. With Thy mysterious fingers dost Thou dress her wounds, and with Thine hands Thou drawest the dread of pain round her pleasures. In her bed Thou hidest pleasure and peace, but beside it Thou dost erect obstacles and fear. Thou dost excite her affection through Thy will, and from her affection does shame emanate. By Thy will Thou showest her the beauty of creation, but her love for beauty becomes a terrible famine. Thou dost make her drink life in the cup of death, and death in the cup of life

Thou purifiest her with tears, and in tears her life streams away. Oh, Lord, Thou hast opened my eyes with love, and with love Thou hast blinded me. Thou hast kissed me with Thy lips and struck me with Thy strong hand. Thou hast planted in my heart a white rose, but around the rose a barrier of thorns. Thou hast tied my present with the spirit of a young man whom I love, but my life with the body of an unknown man. So help me, my Lord, to be strong in this deadly struggle and assist me to be truthful and virtuous until death. Thy will be done, Oh, Lord God."

Silence continued. Selma looked down, pale and frail; her arms dropped, and her head bowed and it seemed to me as if a tempest had broken a branch from a tree and cast it down to dry and perish.

I took her cold hand and kissed it, but when I attempted to console her, it was I who needed consolation more than she did. I kept silent, thinking of our plight and listening to my heartbeats. Neither of us said more.

Extreme torture is mute, and so we sat silent, petrified, like columns of marble buried under the sand of an earthquake. Neither wished to listen to the other because our heart-threads had become weak and even breathing would have broken them.

It was midnight, and we could see the crescent

moon rising from behind Mt. Sunnin, and it looked, in the midst of the stars, like the face of a corpse, in a coffin surrounded by the dim lights of candles. And Lebanon looked like an old man whose back was bent with age and whose eyes were a haven for insomnia, watching the dark and waiting for dawn, like a king sitting on the ashes of his throne in the debris of his palace.

The mountains, trees, and rivers change their appearance with the vicissitudes of times and seasons, as a man changes with his experiences and emotions. The lofty poplar that resembles a bride in the daytime, will look like a column of smoke in the evening; the huge rock that stands impregnable at noon, will appear to be a miserable pauper at night, with earth for his bed and the sky for his cover; and the rivulet that we see glittering in the morning and hear singing the hymn of Eternity, will, in the evening, turn to a stream of tears wailing like a mother bereft of her child, and Lebanon, that had looked dignified a week before, when the moon was full and our spirits were happy, looked sorrowful and lonesome that night.

We stood up and bade each other farewell, but love and despair stood between us like two ghosts, one stretching his wings with his fingers over our throats, one weeping and the other laughing hideously.

As I took Selma's hand and put it to my lips, she came close to me and placed a kiss on my forehead, then dropped on the wooden bench. She shut her eyes and whispered softly, "Oh, Lord God, have mercy on me and mend my broken wings!"

As I left Selma in the garden, I felt as if my senses were covered with a thick veil, like a lake whose surface is concealed by fog.

The beauty of trees, the moonlight, the deep silence, everything about me looked ugly and horrible. The true light that had showed me the beauty and wonder of the universe was converted to a great flame of fire that seared my heart; and the Eternal music I used to hear became a clamor, more frightening than the roar of a lion.

I reached my room, and like a wounded bird shot down by a hunter, I fell on my bed, repeating the words of Selma: "Oh, Lord God, have mercy on me and mend my broken wings!"

7

BEFORE THE THRONE OF DEATH

ARRIAGE IN these days is a mockery whose management is in the hands of young men and parents. In most countries the young men win while the parents lose. The woman is looked upon as a commodity, purchased and delivered from one house to another. In time her beauty fades and she becomes like an old piece of furniture left in a dark corner.

Modern civilization has made woman a little wiser, but it has increased her suffering because of man's covetousness. The woman of yesterday was a happy wife, but the woman of today is a miserable mistress. In the past she walked blindly in the light, but now she walks open-eyed in the dark. She was beautiful in her ignorance, virtuous in her simplicity, and strong in her weakness. Today she has become ugly in her ingenuity, superficial and heartless in her knowledge. Will the day ever come when beauty and knowledge, ingenuity and virtue, and weakness of body and strength of spirit will be united in a woman?

I am one of those who believe that spiritual progress is a rule of human life, but the approach to perfection is slow and painful. If a woman elevates herself in one respect and is retarded in another, it is because the rough trail that leads to the mountain peak is not free of ambushes of thieves and lairs of wolves.

This strange generation exists between sleeping and waking. It holds in its hands the soil of the past and the seeds of the future. However, we find in every city a woman who symbolizes the future.

In the city of Beirut, Selma Karamy was the symbol of the future Oriental woman, but, like many who live ahead of their time, she became the victim of the present; and like a flower snatched from its stem and carried away by the current of a river, she walked in the miserable procession of the defeated.

Mansour Bey Galib and Selma were married, and lived together in a beautiful house at Ras Beyrouth, where all the wealthy dignitaries resided. Farris Effandi Karamy was left in his solitary home in the midst of his garden and orchards like a lonely shepherd amid his flock.

The days and merry nights of the wedding passed, but the honeymoon left memories of times of bitter sorrow, as wars leave skulls and dead bones on the battlefield. The dignity of an Oriental wedding inspires the hearts of young men and women, but its termination may drop them like millstones to the bottom of the sea. Their exhilaration is like footprints on sand which remain only till they are washed away by the waves.

Spring departed, and so did summer and autumn, but my love for Selma increased day by day until it became a kind of mute worship, the feeling that an orphan has toward the soul of his mother in Heaven. My yearning was converted to blind sorrow that could see nothing but itself, and the passion that drew tears from my eyes was replaced by perplexity that sucked the blood from my heart, and my sighs of affection became a constant prayer for the happiness of Selma and her husband and peace for her father.

My hopes and prayers were in vain, because

Selma's misery was an internal malady that nothing but death could cure.

Mansour Bey was a man to whom all the luxuries of life came easily; but, in spite of that, he was dissatisfied and rapacious. After marrying Selma, he neglected her father in his loneliness and prayed for his death so that he could inherit what was left of the old man's wealth.

Mansour Bey's character was similar to his uncle's; the only difference between the two was that the Bishop got everything he wanted secretly, under the protection of his ecclesiastical robe and the golden cross which he wore on his chest, while his nephew did everything publicly. The Bishop went to church in the morning and spent the rest of the day pilfering from the widows, orphans, and simple-minded people. But Mansour Bey spent his days in pursuit of sexual satisfaction. On Sunday, Bishop Bulos Galib preached his Gospel; but during weekdays he never practiced what he preached, occupying himself with the political intrigues of the locality. And, by means of his uncle's prestige and influence, Mansour Bey made it his business to secure political plums for those who could offer a sufficient bribe.

Bishop Bulos was a thief who hid himself under the cover of night, while his nephew, Mansour Bey, was a swindler who walked proudly in daylight.

However, the people of Oriental nations place trust in such as they—wolves and butchers who ruin their country through covetousness and crush their neighbors with an iron hand.

Why do I occupy these pages with words about the betrayers of poor nations instead of reserving all the space for the story of a miserable woman with a broken heart? Why do I shed tears for oppressed peoples rather than keep all my tears for the memory of a weak woman whose life was snatched by the teeth of death?

But my dear readers, don't you think that such a woman is like a nation that is oppressed by priests and rulers? Don't you believe that thwarted love which leads a woman to the grave is like the despair which pervades the people of the earth? A woman is to a nation as light is to a lamp. Will not the light be dim if the oil in the lamp is low?

Autumn passed, and the wind blew the yellow leaves from the trees, making way for winter, which came howling and crying. I was still in the City of Beirut without a companion save my dreams, which would lift my spirit to the sky and then bury it deep in the bosom of the earth.

The sorrowful spirit finds relaxation in solitude. It abhors people, as a wounded deer deserts the herd and lives in a cave until it is healed or dead.

One day I heard that Farris Effandi was ill. I left my solitary abode and walked to his home, taking a new route, a lonely path between olive trees, avoiding the main road with its rattling carriage wheels.

Arriving at the old man's house, I entered and found Farris Effandi lying on his bed, weak and pale. His eyes were sunken and looked like two deep, dark valleys haunted by the ghosts of pain. The smile which had always enlivened his face was choked with pain and agony; and the bones of his gentle hands looked like naked branches trembling before the tempest. As I approached him and inquired as to his health, he turned his pale face toward me, and on his trembling lips appeared a smile, and he said in a weak voice, "Go—go, my son, to the other room and comfort Selma and bring her to sit by the side of my bed."

I entered the adjacent room and found Selma lying on a divan, covering her head with her arms and burying her face in a pillow so that her father would not hear her weeping. Approaching slowly, I pronounced her name in a voice that seemed more like sighing than whispering. She moved fearfully, as if she had been interrupted in a terrible dream, and sat up, looking at me with glazed eyes, doubting whether I was a ghost or a living being. After a deep silence which took us back on the wings of memory to that hour when we were intoxicated with the wine of love, Selma wiped away her tears and said, "See how time has changed us! See how time has changed the course of our lives and left us in these ruins. In this place spring united us in a bond of love, and in this place has brought us together before the throne of death. How beautiful was spring, and how terrible is this winter!"

Speaking thus, she covered her face again with her hands as if she were shielding her eyes from the spectre of the past standing before her. I put my hand on her head and said, "Come, Selma, come and let us be as strong towers before the tempest. Let us stand like brave soldiers before the enemy and face his weapons. If we are killed, we shall die as martyrs; and if we win, we shall live as heroes. Braving obstacles and hardships is nobler than retreat to tranquility. The butterfly that hovers around the lamp until it dies is more admirable than the mole that lives in a dark tunnel. Come, Selma, let us walk this rough path firmly, with our eyes toward the sun so that we may not see the skulls and serpents among the rocks and thorns. If fear should stop us in the middle of the road, we would hear only ridicule from the voices of the night, but if we reach the mountain peak bravely we shall join the heavenly spirits in songs of triumph and joy. Cheer up, Selma, wipe away your tears and remove the sorrow from your face. Rise, and let us sit by the bed of your father, because his life depends on your life, and your smile is his only cure."

Kindly and affectionately she looked at me and said, "Are you asking me to have patience, while you are in need of it yourself? Will a hungry man give his bread to another hungry man? Or will a sick man give medicine to another which he himself needs badly?"

She rose, her head bent slightly forward, and we walked to the old man's room and sat by the side of his bed. Selma forced a smile and pretended to be patient, and her father tried to make her believe that he was feeling better and getting stronger; but both father and daughter were aware of each other's sorrow and heard the unvoiced sighs. They were like two equal forces, wearing each other away silently. The father's heart was melting because of his daughter's plight. They were two pure souls, one departing and the other agonized with grief, embracing in love and death; and I was between the two with my own troubled heart. We were three people, gathered and crushed by the hands of destiny; an old man like a dwelling ruined by flood, a young woman whose symbol was a lily beheaded by the sharp edge of a sickle, and a young man who was a weak sapling, bent by a snowfall; and all of us were toys in the hands of fate.

Farris Effandi moved slowly and stretched his weak hand toward Selma, and in a loving and tender voice said, "Hold my hand, my beloved." Selma held his hand; then he said, "I have lived long enough, and I have enjoyed the fruits of life's seasons. I nave experienced all its phases with equanimity. I lost your mother when you were three years of age, and she left you as a precious treasure in my lap. I watched you grow, and your face reproduced your mother's features as stars reflected in a calm pool of water. Your character, intelligence, and beauty are your mother's, even your manner of speaking and gestures. You have been my only consolation in this life because you were the image of your mother in every deed and word. Now, I grow old, and my only resting place is between the soft wings of death. Be comforted, my beloved daughter, because I have lived long enough to see you as a woman. Be happy because I shall live in you after my death. My departure today would be no different from my going tomorrow or the day after, for our days are perishing like the leaves of autumn. The hour of my death approaches rapidly, and my soul is desirous of being united with your mother's."

As he uttered these words sweetly and lovingly,

his face was radiant Then he put his hand under his pillow and pulled out a small picture in a gold frame. With his eyes on the little photograph, he said, "Come, Selma, come and see your mother in this picture."

Selma wiped away her tears, and after gazing long at the picture, she kissed it repeatedly and cried, "Oh, my beloved mother! Oh, mother!" Then she placed her trembling lips on the picture as if she wished to pour her soul into that image.

The most beautiful word on the lips of mankind is the word "Mother," and the most beautiful call is the call of "My mother." It is a word full of hope and love, a sweet and kind word coming from the depths of the heart. The mother is every thing—she is our consolation in sorrow, our hope in misery, and our strength in weakness. She is the source of love, mercy, sympathy, and forgiveness. He who loses his mother loses a pure soul who blesses and guards him constantly.

Every thing in nature bespeaks the mother. The sun is the mother of earth and gives it its nourishment of heat; it never leaves the universe at night until it has put the earth to sleep to the song of the sea and the hymn of birds and brooks. And this earth is the mother of trees and flowers. It produces them, nurses them, and weans them. The trees and flowers become kind mothers of their great fruits and seeds. And the mother, the prototype of all existence, is the eternal spirit, full of beauty and love.

Selma Karamy never knew her mother because she had died when Selma was an infant, but Selma wept when she saw the picture and cried, "Oh, mother!" The word mother is hidden in our hearts, and it comes upon our lips in hours of sorrow and happiness as the perfume comes from the heart of the rose and mingles with clear and cloudy air.

Selma stared at her mother's picture, kissing it repeatedly, until she collapsed by her father's bed.

The old man placed both hands on her head and said, "I have shown you, my dear child, a picture of your mother on paper. Now listen to me and I shall let you hear her words."

She lifted her head like a little bird in the nest that hears its mother's wing, and looked at him attentively.

Farris Effandi opened his mouth and said, "Your mother was nursing you when she lost her father; she cried and wept at his going, but she was wise and patient. She sat by me in this room as soon as the funeral was over and held my hand and said, 'Farris, my father is dead now and you are my only consolation in this world. The heart's affections are divided like the branches of the cedar tree; if the tree loses one strong branch, it will suffer but it does not die. It will pour all its vitality into the next branch so that it will grow and fill the empty place.' This is what your mother told me when her father died, and you should say the same thing when death takes my body to its resting place and my soul to God's care."

Selma answered him with falling tears and broken heart, "When Mother lost her father, you took his place; but who is going to take yours when you are gone? She was left in the care of a loving and truthful husband; she found consolation in her little daughter, and who will be my consolation when you pass away? You have been my father and mother and the companion of my youth."

Saying these words, she turned and looked at me, and, holding the side of my garment, said, "This is the only friend I shall have after you are gone, but how can he console me when he is suffering also? How can a broken heart find consolation in a disappointed soul? A sorrowful woman cannot be comforted by her neighbor's sorrow, nor can a bird fly with broken wings. He is the friend of my soul, but I have already placed a heavy burden of sorrow upon him and dimmed his eyes with my tears till he can see nothing but darkness. He is a brother whom I dearly love, but he is like all brothers who share my

94

sorrow and help me shed tears which increase my bitterness and burn my heart."

Selma's words stabbed my heart, and I felt that I could bear no more. The old man listened to her with depressed spirit, trembling like the light of a lamp before the wind. Then he stretched out his hand and said, "Let me go peacefully, my child. I have broken the bars of this cage; let me fly and do not stop me, for your mother is calling me. The sky is clear and the sea is calm and the boat is ready to sail; do not delay its voyage. Let my body rest with those who are resting; let my dream end and my soul awaken with the dawn; let your soul embrace mine and give me the kiss of hope; let no drops of sorrow or bitterness fall upon my body lest the flowers and grass refuse their nourishment. Do not shed tears of misery upon my hand, for they may grow thorns upon my grave. Do not draw lines of agony upon my forehead, for the wind may pass and read them and refuse to carry the dust of my bones to the green prairies . . . I loved you, my child, while I lived, and I shall love you when I am dead, and my soul shall always watch over you and protect you."

Then Farris Effandi looked at me with his eyes half closed and said, "My son, be a real brother to Selma as your father was to me. Be her help and friend in need, and do not let her mourn, because mourning for the dead is a mistake. Repeat to her pleasant tales and sing for her the songs of life so that she may forget her sorrows. Remember me to your father; ask him to tell you the stories of our youth and tell him that I loved him in the person of his son in the last hour of my life."

Silence prevailed, and I could see the pallor of death on the old man's face. Then he rolled his eyes and looked at us and whispered, "Don't call the physician, for he might extend my sentence in this prison by his medicine. The days of slavery are gone, and my soul seeks the freedom of the skies. And do not call the priest to my bedside, because his incantations would not save me if I were a sinner, nor would it rush me to Heaven if I were innocent. The will of humanity cannot change the will of God, as an astrologer cannot change the course of the stars. But after my death let the doctors and priest do what they please, for my ship will continue sailing until it reaches its destination."

At midnight Farris Effandi opened his tired eyes for the last time and focused them on Selma, who was kneeling by his bedside. He tried to speak, but could not, for death had already choked his voice; but he finally managed to say, "The night has passed

. . . Oh, Selma . . . Oh . . . Oh, Selma . . ." Then he bent his head, his face turned white, and I could see a smile on his lips as he breathed his last.

Selma felt her father's hand. It was cold. Then she raised her head and looked at his face. It was covered with the veil of death. Selma was so choked that she could not shed tears, nor sigh, nor even move. For a moment she stared at him with fixed eyes like those of a statue; then she bent down until her forehead touched the floor, and said, "Oh, Lord, have mercy and mend our broken wings."

Farris Effandi Karamy died; his soul was embraced by Eternity, and his body was returned to the earth. Mansour Bey Galib got possession of his wealth, and Selma became a prisoner for life—a life of grief and misery.

I was lost in sorrow and reverie. Days and nights preyed upon me as the eagle ravages its victim. Many a time I tried to forget my misfortune by occupying myself with books and scriptures of past generations, but it was like extinguishing fire with oil, for I could see nothing in the procession of the past but tragedy and could hear nothing but weeping and wailing. The Book of Job was more fascinating to me than the Psalms and I preferred the Elegies of Jeremiah to the Song of Solomon. *Hamlet* was closer to my heart than all other dramas of western writers. Thus despair weakens our sight and closes our ears. We can see nothing but spectres of doom, and can hear only the beating of our agitated hearts.

8

BETWEEN CHRIST AND ISHTAR

I N THE MIDST OF
the gardens and hills which connect the city of Beirut
with Lebanon there is a small temple, very ancient,
dug out of white rock, surrounded by olive, almond,
and willow trees. Although this temple is a half mile
from the main highway, at the time of my story very
few people interested in relics and ancient ruins had
visited it. It was one of many interesting places hidden and forgotten in Lebanon. Due to its seclusion,
it had become a haven for worshipers and a shrine for
lonely lovers.

As one enters this temple he sees on the wall at
the east side an old Phoenician picture, carved in the

rock, depicting Ishtar, goddess of love and beauty, sitting on her throne, surrounded by seven nude virgins standing in different poses. The first one carries a torch; the second, a guitar; the third, a censer; the fourth, a jug of wine; the fifth, a branch of roses; the sixth, a wreath of laurel; the seventh, a bow and arrow; and all of them look at Ishtar reverently.

On the second wall there is another picture, more modern than the first one, symbolizing Christ nailed to the cross, and at His side stand His sorrowful mother and Mary Magdalene and two other women weeping. This Byzantine picture shows that it was carved in the fifteenth or sixteenth century.*

On the west side wall there are two round transits through which the sun's rays enter the temple and strike the pictures and make them look as if they were painted with gold water color. In the middle of the temple there is a square marble with old paintings on its sides, some of which can hardly be seen under the petrified lumps of blood which show that the ancient people offered sacrifices on this rock and poured perfume, wine, and oil upon it.

There is nothing else in that little temple except deep silence, revealing to the living the secrets of the

* It is known by the students of relics that most of the Christian churches in the East were temples for the old Phoenician and Greek gods. In Damascus, Antioch and Constantinople, there are many edifices, the walls of which echoed heathen hymns; these places were converted into churches and then into mosques.

goddess and speaking wordlessly of past generations and the evolution of religions. Such a sight carries the poet to a world far away from the one in which he dwells and convinces the philosopher that men were born religious; they felt a need for that which they could not see and drew symbols, the meaning of which divulged their hidden secrets and their desires in life and death.

In that unknown temple, I met Selma once every month and spent the hours with her, looking at those strange pictures, thinking of the crucified Christ and pondering upon the young Phoenician men and women who lived, loved and worshipped beauty in the person of Ishtar by burning incense before her statue and pouring perfume on her shrine, people for whom nothing is left to speak except the name, repeated by the march of time before the face of Eternity.

It is hard to write down in words the memories of those hours when I met Selma—those heavenly hours, filled with pain, happiness, sorrow, hope, and misery.

We met secretly in the old temple, remembering the old days, discussing our present, fearing our future, and gradually bringing out the hidden secrets in the depths of our hearts and complaining to each other of our misery and suffering, trying to console ourselves with imaginary hopes and sorrowful dreams. Every now and then we would become calm and wipe our tears and start smiling, forgetting everything except Love; we embraced each other until our hearts melted; then Selma would print a pure kiss on my forehead and fill my heart with ecstasy; I would return the kiss as she bent her ivory neck while her cheeks became gently red like the first ray of dawn on the forehead of hills. We silently looked at the distant horizon where the clouds were colored with the orange ray of sunset.

Our conversation was not limited to love; every now and then we drifted on to current topics and exchanged ideas. During the course of conversation Selma spoke of woman's place in society, the imprint that the past generation had left on her character, the relationship between husband and wife, and the spiritual diseases and corruption which threatened married life. I remember her saying: "The poets and writers are trying to understand the reality of woman, but up to this day they have not understood the hidden secrets of her heart, because they look upon her from behind the sexual veil and see nothing but externals; they look upon her through a magnifying glass of hatefulness and find nothing except weakness and submission."

On another occasion she said, pointing to the

104

carved pictures on the walls of the temple, "In the heart of this rock there are two symbols depicting the essence of a woman's desires and revealing the hidden secrets of her soul, moving between love and sorrow—between affection and sacrifice, between Ishtar sitting on the throne and Mary standing by the cross. The man buys glory and reputation, but the woman pays the price."

No one knew about our secret meetings except God and the flock of birds which flew over the temple. Selma used to come in her carriage to a place named Pasha Park and from there she walked to the temple, where she found me anxiously waiting for her.

We feared not the observer's eyes, neither did our consciences bother us; the spirit which is purified by fire and washed by tears is higher than what the people call shame and disgrace; it is free from the laws of slavery and old customs against the affections of the human heart. That spirit can proudly stand unashamed before the throne of God.

Human society has yielded for seventy centuries to corrupted laws until it cannot understand the meaning of the superior and eternal laws. A man's eyes have become accustomed to the dim light of candles and cannot see the sunlight. Spiritual disease is inherited from one generation to another until it has become a part of the people, who look upon it, not as a disease, but as a natural gift, showered by God upon Adam. If those people found someone free from the germs of this disease, they would think of him with shame and disgrace.

Those who think evil of Selma Karamy because she left her husband's home and met me in the temple are the diseased and weak-minded kind who look upon the healthy and sound as rebels. They are like insects crawling in the dark for fear of being stepped upon by the passers-by.

The oppressed prisoner, who can break away from his jail and does not do so, is a coward. Selma, an innocent and oppressed prisoner, was unable to free herself from slavery. Was she to blame because she looked through the jail window upon the green fields and spacious sky? Will the people count her as being untruthful to her husband because she came from his home to sit by me between Christ and Ishtar? Let the people say what they please; Selma had passed the marshes which submerge other spirits and had landed in a world that could not be reached by the howling of wolves and rattling of snakes. People may say what they want about me, for the spirit who has seen the spectre of death cannot be scared by the faces of thieves; the soldier who has seen the swords glittering over his head and streams of blood under his feet does not care about rocks thrown at him by the children on the streets.

9

THE SACRIFICE

ONE DAY IN THE LATE part of June, as the people left the city for the mountain to avoid the heat of summer, I went as usual to the temple to meet Selma, carrying with me a little book of Andalusian poems. As I reached the temple I sat there waiting for Selma, glancing at intervals at the pages of my book, reciting those verses which filled my heart with ecstasy and brought to my soul the memory of the kings, poets, and knights who bade farewell to Granada, and left, with tears in their eyes and sorrow in their hearts, their palaces, institutions and hopes behind. In an hour I saw Selma walking in the midst of the gardens and approaching the temple, leaning on her parasol as if she were carrying all the worries of the world upon her shoulders. As she entered the temple and sat by me, I noticed some sort of change in her eyes and I was anxious to inquire about it.

Selma felt what was going on in my mind, and she put her hand on my head and said, "Come close to me, come my beloved, come and let me quench my thirst, for the hour of separation has come."

I asked her, "Did your husband find out about our meetings here?" She responded, "My husband does not care about me, neither does he know how I spend my time, for he is busy with those poor girls whom poverty has driven into the houses of ill fame; those girls who sell their bodies for bread, kneaded with blood and tears."

I inquired, "What prevents you from coming to this temple and sitting by me reverently before God? Is your soul requesting our separation?"

She answered with tears in her eyes, "No, my beloved, my spirit did not ask for separation, for you are a part of me: My eyes never get tired of looking at you, for you are their light; but if destiny ruled that I should walk the rough path of life loaded with shackles, would I be satisfied if your fate should be like mine?" Then she added, "I cannot say everything, because the tongue is mute with pain and cannot talk; the lips are sealed with misery and cannot move; all I can say to you is that I am afraid you may fall in the same trap I fell in."

Then I asked, "What do you mean, Selma, and of whom are you afraid?" She covered her face with her hands and said, "The Bishop has already found out that once a month I have been leaving the grave which he buried me in."

I inquired, "Did the Bishop find out about our meetings here?" She answered, "If he did, you would not see me here sitting by you; but he is getting suspicious and he informed all his servants and guards to watch me closely. I am feeling that the house I live in and the path I walk on are all eyes watching me, and fingers pointing at me, and ears listening to the whisper of my thoughts."

She was silent for a while, and then she added, with tears pouring down her cheeks, "I am not afraid of the Bishop, for wetness does not scare the drowned, but I am afraid you might fall into the trap and become his prey; you are still young and free as the sunlight. I am not frightened of fate which has shot all its arrows in my breast, but I am afraid the serpent might bite your feet and detain you from climbing the mountain peak where the future awaits you with its pleasure and glory."

I said, "He who has not been bitten by the serpents of light and snapped at by the wolves of darkness will always be deceived by the days and nights. But listen, Selma, listen carefully; is separation the only means of avoiding people's evils and meanness? Has the path of love and freedom been closed and is nothing left except submission to the will of the slaves of death?"

She responded, "Nothing is left save separation and bidding each other farewell."

With rebellious spirit I took her hand and said excitedly, "We have yielded to the people's will for a long time; since the time we met until this hour we have been led by the blind and have worshipped with them before their idols. Since the time I met you we have been in the hands of the Bishop like two balls which he has thrown around as he pleased. Are we going to submit to his will until death takes us away? Did God give us the breath of life to place it under death's feet? Did He give us liberty to make it a shadow for slavery? He who extinguishes his spirit's fire with his own hands is an infidel in the eyes of Heaven, for Heaven set the fire that burns in our spirits. He who does not rebel against oppression is doing himself injustice. I love you, Selma, and you love me, too; and Love is a precious treasure, it is God's gift to sensitive and great spirits. Shall we throw this treasure away and let the pigs scatter it and trample on it? This world is full of wonder and beauty. Why are we living in this narrow tunnel which the Bishop and his assistants have dug out for us? Life is full of happiness and freedom; why don't we take this heavy yoke off our shoulders and break the chains tied to our feet, and walk freely toward peace? Get up and let us leave this small temple for God's great temple. Let us leave this country and all its slavery and ignorance for another country far away and unreached by the hands of the thieves. Let us go to the coast under the cover of night and catch a boat that will take us across the oceans, where we can find a new life full of happiness and understanding. Do not hesitate, Selma, for these minutes are more precious to us than the crowns of kings and more sublime than the thrones of angels. Let us follow the column of light that leads us from this arid desert into the green fields where flowers and aromatic plants grow."

She shook her head and gazed at something invisible on the ceiling of the temple; a sorrowful smile appeared on her lips; then she said, "No, no my beloved. Heaven placed in my hand a cup, full of vinegar and gall; I forced myself to drink it in order to know the full bitterness at the bottom until nothing was left save a few drops, which I shall drink patiently I am not worthy of a new life of love and peace; I am not strong enough for life's pleasure and sweetness, because a bird with broken wings cannot fly in the spacious sky. The eyes that are accustomed to the dim light of a candle are not strong enough to stare at the sun. Do not talk to me of happiness; its memory makes me suffer. Mention not peace to me; its shadow frightens me; but look at me and I will show you the holy torch which Heaven has lighted in the ashes of my heart —you know that I love you as a mother loves her only child, and Love only taught me to protect you even from myself. It is Love, purified with fire, that stops me from following you to the farthest land. Love kills my desires so that you may live freely and virtuously. Limited love asks for possession of the beloved, but the unlimited asks only for itself. Love that comes between the naiveté and awakening of youth satisfies itself with possessing, and grows with embraces. But Love which is born in the firmament's lap and has descended with the night's secrets is not contented with anything but Eternity and immortality; it does not stand reverently before anything except deity.

"When I knew that the Bishop wanted to stop me from leaving his nephew's house and to take my only pleasure away from me, I stood before the window of my room and looked toward the sea, thinking of the vast countries beyond it and the real freedom and personal independence which can be found there. I felt that I was living close to you, surrounded by the shadow of your spirit, submerged in the ocean of your affection. But all these thoughts which illuminate a woman's heart and make her rebel against old customs and live in the shadow of freedom and justice, made me believe that I am weak and that our love is limited and feeble, unable to stand before the sun's face. I cried like a king whose kingdom and treasures have been usurped, but immediately I saw your face through my tears and your eyes gazing at me and I remembered what you said to me once (*Come, Selma, come and let us be strong towers before the tempest. Let us stand like brave soldiers before the enemy and face his weapons. If we are killed, we shall die as martyrs; and if we win, we shall live as heroes. Braving obstacles and hardships is nobler than retreat to tranquility.*) These words, my beloved, you uttered when the wings of death were hovering around my father's bed; I remembered them yesterday when the wings of despair were hovering above my head. I strengthened myself and felt, while in the darkness of my prison, some sort of precious freedom easing our difficulties and diminishing our sorrows. I found out that our love was as deep as the ocean and as high as the stars and as spacious as the sky. I came here to see you, and in my weak spirit there is a new strength, and this strength is the ability to sacrifice a great thing in order to obtain a greater one; it is the sacrifice of my happiness so that you may remain virtuous and honorable in the eyes of the people and be far away from their treachery and persecution . . .

"In the past, when I came to this place I felt as if heavy chains were pulling down on me, but today I came here with a new determination that laughs at the shackles and shortens the way. I used to come to this temple like a scared phantom, but today I came like a brave woman who feels the urgency of sacrifice and knows the value of suffering, a woman who likes to protect the one she loves from the ignorant people and from her hungry spirit. I used to sit by you like a trembling shadow, but today I came here to show you my true self before Ishtar and Christ.

"I am a tree, grown in the shade, and today I stretched my branches to tremble for a while in the daylight. I came here to tell you good-bye, my beloved, and it is my hope that our farewell will be great and awful like our love. Let our farewell be like fire that bends the gold and makes it more resplendent."

Selma did not allow me to speak or protest, but she looked at me, her eyes glittering, her face retaining its dignity, seeming like an angel worthy of silence and respect. Then she flung herself upon me, something which she had never done before, and put her smooth arms around me and printed a long, deep, fiery kiss on my lips.

As the sun went down, withdrawing its rays from those gardens and orchards, Selma moved to the middle of the temple and gazed long at its walls and corners as if she wanted to pour the light of her eyes on its pictures and symbols. Then she walked forward and reverently knelt before the picture of Christ and kissed His feet, and she whispered, "Oh, Christ, I have chosen Thy Cross and deserted Ishtar's world of pleasure and happiness; I have worn the wreath of thorns and discarded the wreath of laurel and washed myself with blood and tears instead of perfume and scent; I have drunk vinegar and gall from a cup which was meant for wine and nectar; accept me, my Lord, among Thy followers and lead me toward Galilee with those who have chosen Thee, contented with their sufferings and delighted with their sorrows."

Then she rose and looked at me and said, "Now I shall return happily to my dark cave, where horrible ghosts reside. Do not sympathize with me, my beloved, and do not feel sorry for me, because the soul that sees the shadow of God once will never be frightened, thereafter, of the ghosts of devils. And the eye that looks on Heaven once will not be closed by the pains of the world."

Uttering these words, Selma left the place of worship; and I remained there lost in a deep sea of thoughts, absorbed in the world of revelation where God sits on the throne and the angels write down the acts of human beings, and the souls recite the tragedy of life, and the brides of Heaven sing the hymns of love, sorrow and immortality.

Night had already come when I awakened from my swoon and found myself bewildered in the midst of the gardens, repeating the echo of every word uttered by Selma and remembering her silence, her actions, her movements, her expressions and the touch of her hands, until I realized the meaning of farewell and the pain of lonesomeness. I was depressed and heart-broken. It was my first discovery of the fact that men, even if they are born free, will remain slaves of strict laws enacted by their forefathers; and that the firmament, which we imagine as unchanging, is the yielding of today to the will of tomorrow and submission of yesterday to the will of today—Many a time, since that night, I have thought of the spiritual law which made Selma prefer death to life, and many a time I have made a comparison between nobility of sacrifice and happiness of rebellion to find out which one is nobler and more beautiful; but until now I have distilled only one truth out of the whole matter, and this truth is *sincerity*, which makes all our deeds beautiful and honorable And this *sincerity* was in Selma Karamy.

THE RESCUER

IVE YEARS OF SELMA'S
marriage passed without bringing children to
strengthen the ties of spiritual relation between her
and her husband and bind their repugnant souls
together.

A barren woman is looked upon with disdain
everywhere because of most men's desire to per-
petuate themselves through posterity.

The substantial man considers his childless wife
as an enemy; he detests her and deserts her and
wishes her death. Mansour Bey Galib was that kind

of man; materially, he was like earth, and hard like steel and greedy like a grave. His desire of having a child to carry on his name and reputation made him hate Selma in spite of her beauty and sweetness.

A tree grown in a cave does not bear fruit; and Selma, who lived in the shade of life, did not bear children. . . .

The nightingale does not make his nest in a cage lest slavery be the lot of its chicks. . . . Selma was a prisoner of misery and it was Heaven's will that she would not have another prisoner to share her life. The flowers of the field are the children of sun's affection and nature's love; and the children of men are the flowers of love and compassion. . . .

The spirit of love and compassion never dominated Selma's beautiful home at Ras Beyrouth; nevertheless, she knelt down on her knees every night before Heaven and asked God for a child in whom she would find comfort and consolation. . . . She prayed successively until Heaven answered her prayers. . . .

The tree of the cave blossomed to bear fruit at last. The nightingale in the cage commenced making its nest with the feathers of its wings.

Selma stretched her chained arms toward Heaven to receive God's precious gift and nothing in the world could have made her happier than becoming a potential mother. . . .

She waited anxiously, counting the days and looking forward to the time when Heaven's sweetest melody, the voice of her child, should ring in her ears. . . .

She commenced to see the dawn of a brighter future through her tears. . . .

It was in the month of Nisan when Selma was stretched on the bed of pain and labor, where life and death were wrestling. The doctor and the midwife were ready to deliver to the world a new guest. Late at night Selma started her successive cry . . . a cry of life's partition from life . . . a cry of continuance in the firmament of nothingness . . . a cry of a weak force before the stillness of great forces . . . the cry of poor Selma who was lying down in despair under the feet of life and death.

At dawn Selma gave birth to a baby boy. When she opened her eyes she saw smiling faces all over the room, then she looked again and saw life and death still wrestling by her bed. She closed her eyes and cried, saying for the first time, "Oh, my son." The midwife wrapped the infant with silk swaddles and placed him by his mother, but the doctor kept looking at Selma and sorrowfully shaking his head.

123

The voices of joy woke the neighbors, who rushed into the house to felicitate the father upon the birth of his heir, but the doctor still gazed at Selma and her infant and shook his head. . . .

The servants hurried to spread the good news to Mansour Bey, but the doctor stared at Selma and her child with a disappointed look on his face.

As the sun came out, Selma took the infant to her breast; he opened his eyes for the first time and looked at his mother; then he quivered and closed them for the last time. The doctor took the child from Selma's arms, and on his cheeks fell tears; then he whispered to himself, "He is a departing guest."

The child passed away while the neighbors were celebrating with the father in the big hall at the house and drinking to the health of the heir; and Selma looked at the doctor, and pleaded, "Give me my child and let me embrace him."

Though the child was dead, the sounds of the drinking cups increased in the hall. . . .

He was born at dawn and died at sunrise. . . .

He was born like a thought and died like a sigh and disappeared like a shadow.

He did not live to console and comfort his mother.

His life began at the end of the night and ended at the beginning of the day, like a drop of dew poured by the eyes of the dark and dried by the touch of the light.

A pearl brought by the tide to the coast and returned by the ebb into the depth of the sea. . . .

A lily that has just blossomed from the bud of life and is mashed under the feet of death.

A dear guest whose appearance illuminated Selma's heart and whose departure killed her soul.

This is the life of men, the life of nations, the life of suns, moons and stars.

And Selma focused her eyes upon the doctor and cried, "Give me my child and let me embrace him; give me my child and let me nurse him."

Then the doctor bent his head. His voice choked and he said, "Your child is dead, Madame, be patient."

Upon hearing the doctor's announcement, Selma uttered a terrible cry. Then she was quiet for a moment and smiled happily. Her face brightened as if she had discovered something, and quietly she said, "Give me my child; bring him close to me and let me see him dead."

The doctor carried the dead child to Selma and placed him between her arms. She embraced him, then turned her face toward the wall and addressed the dead infant saying, "You have come to take me away, my child; you have come to show me`the way that leads to the coast. Here I am, my child; lead me and let us leave this dark cave."

And in a minute the sun's ray penetrated the window curtains and fell upon two calm bodies lying on a bed, guarded by the profound dignity of silence and shaded by the wings of death. The doctor left the room with tears in his eyes, and as he reached the big hall the celebration was converted into a funeral, but Mansour Bey Galib never uttered a word or shed a tear. He remained standing motionless like a statue, holding a drinking cup with his right hand.

· · · · ·

The second day Selma was shrouded with her white wedding dress and laid in a coffin; the child's shroud was his swaddle; his coffin was his mother's arms; his grave was her calm breast. Two corpses were carried in one coffin, and I walked reverently with the crowd accompanying Selma and her infant to their resting place.

Arriving at the cemetery, Bishop Galib commenced chanting while the other priests prayed, and on their gloomy faces appeared a veil of ignorance and emptiness.

As the coffin went down, one of the bystanders whispered, "This is the first time in my life I have

126

seen two corpses in one coffin." Another one said, "It seems as if the child had come to rescue his mother from her pitiless husband."

A third one said, "Look at Mansour Bey: he is gazing at the sky as if his eyes were made of glass. He does not look like he has lost his wife and child in one day." A fourth one added, "His uncle, the Bishop, will marry him again tomorrow to a wealthier and stronger woman."

The Bishop and the priests kept on singing and chanting until the grave digger was through filling the ditch. Then, the people, individually, approached the Bishop and his nephew and offered their respects to them with sweet words of sympathy, but I stood lonely aside without a soul to console me, as if Selma and her child meant nothing to me.

The farewell-bidders left the cemetery; the grave digger stood by the new grave holding a shovel with his hand.

As I approached him, I inquired, "Do you remember where Farris Effandi Karamy was buried?"

He looked at me for a moment, then pointed at Selma's grave and said, "Right here; I placed his daughter upon him and upon his daughter's breast rests her child, and upon all I put the earth back with this shovel."

Then I said, "In this ditch you have also buried my heart."

As the grave digger disappeared behind the poplar trees, I could not resist any more; I dropped down on Selma's grave and wept.